THE FIRST MUSIC

AS TOLD BY
DYLAN PRITCHETT

ILLUSTRATED BY
Erin Bennett Banks

AUGUST HOUSE
Little folk

LITTLE ROCK

Published 2006 by August House Publishers, Inc.
P.O. Box 3223, Little Rock, Arkansas, 72203,
501–372–5450
http://www.augusthouse.com

Manufactured in Korea
Book design by Liz Lester

10   9   8   7   6   5   4   3   2   1

LIBRARY OF CONGRESS CATALOGING-IN-PUBLICATION DATA

Pritchett, Dylan, 1959–
    The first music / Dylan Pritchett ; illustrated by Erin Bennett Banks.
       p.   cm.
    Summary: A series of accidents in the jungle proves that everyone
has something special to add when it comes to making music.
    ISBN-13: 978-0-87483-776-6 (hardcover : alk. paper)
    ISBN-10: 0-87483-776-6 (hardcover : alk. paper)
    [1. Music–Fiction. 2. Jungle animals–Fiction.] I. Banks, Erin
Bennett, ill. II. Title.

    PZ7.P94133Fir   2006
    [E]–dc22
                                          2006042708

The paper used in this publication meets the minimum requirements
of the American National Standard for Information Sciences—
Permanence of Paper for Printed Library Materials,
ANSI Z39.48–1984.

AUGUST HOUSE PUBLISHERS   LITTLE ROCK

To my family:
Wife, Buddy, and Boojie.

Also to the "Blue Man" who brings me
wisdom through the heart and ear, then
weaves it into the stories I share.—DP

To Madeline Joy, with love—EBB

In the beginning,
the African forest had many sounds.

Hyena yelped.

Owl hooted.

Buffalo groaned.

Parrot screeched.

Monkey chittered.

Crocodile snorted.

Padada-
pada-pada

Only the
frogs were silent.

*Padada-pada-
padada-
pada*

Suddenly a noise
like thunder rolled
through the air.

BOOM! BOOM! BOOM! BOOM!
Padada BOOM!

The animals stopped talking.

Hyena peered over the grass.

Buffalo raised his head from
the stream.

Parrot turned her head from
side to side, looking for
the noisemaker.

Monkey leapt from tree to tree,
following the sound. He found Elephant
rubbing his back foot with his front one.

"Who made that loud noise?" Monkey asked.

"Me!" Elephant moaned.
"I stubbed my foot on this hollow log."
Elephant started beating the log with his front foot.

BOOM!
Padada BOOM—
pada BOOM—
padada BOOM—
pada BOOM!

Other animals
   began to gather
around.

"I like that sound,"
   said Elephant.

He kept up the beat.

Padada BOOM—pada BOOM—
padada BOOM—pada BOOM!

Monkey listened to the rhythm.
"I feel like moving!" he said.

Monkey began to sway back and forth.
The leaves rustled as the branches
rubbed together.

Shh-ka-shh! Shh-ka-shh!
Shh-ka-shh! Shh-ka-shh!

Elephant pounded
while Monkey danced.
Such a pair!

Padada BOOM—pada BOOM—
padada BOOM—pada BOOM!

Shh-ka-shh! Shh-ka-shh!
Shh-ka-shh! Shh-ka-shh!

Crocodile raised his body out of the water.
Crane flew down and perched on Crocodile's back.

"Look at Monkey jumping up and down,"
Crocodile snorted.

"It looks like fun. It sounds like fun, too,"
Crane crooned.

Crane began rocking back and forth.
Crocodile shifted his body.
Crane lost her balance and slid.
Her sharp claws tinkled over the scales on
Crocodile's back.

Skee-de-lee! Kee-key-key!
Skee-de-lee! Kee-key-key!

"Hey, that tickles!" said Crocodile.

Elephant beat on the log.

Monkey danced.

Crane played Crocodile's scales.

Hyena yelped.

Owl whooed.

Buffalo bellowed.

And Parrot screeched along in rhythm.

The frogs kept silent.
Parrot flew over and landed next to them.
"Why don't you join in?" she asked.

"We have short legs and cannot dance,"
King Frog replied. "We have short hands
and cannot play.

There is nothing for us
to do but watch and listen."

*Padada BOOM—pada BOOM—
padada BOOM—pada BOOM!*

*Shh-ka-shh! Shh-ka-shh!
Shh-ka-shh! Shh-ka-shh!*

*Skee-de-lee! Kee-key-key!
Skee-de-lee! Kee-key-key!*

One by one, and two by two, more animals gathered.

Lioness groaned and moaned.

Hawk slapped and flapped his wings.

Together they played and swayed
and danced and pranced.

*Padada BOOM—pada BOOM—
padada BOOM—pada BOOM!*

The frogs remained silent.

The animals danced and played

the first day while the frogs watched.

They pranced and swayed the second day,
and the frogs listened.

The third,
    fourth,
        fifth, and
            sixth days,
            they danced and
            played so hard that
            the earth shook.

Except
the frogs,

who went to their pond
to ponder.

At dawn on the seventh day,
all was quiet.

The animals had decided to rest.
They returned to their homes.

Suddenly, from the pond, a new sound
echoed through the forest.

Reep-reep-ree!
Reep-reep-ree!
Reep-reep-ree!

"What is that?" Crocodile asked.

The animals went to the pond.

There, gathered on a stage of
lily pads, the frogs sang proudly.

Reep-reep-ree!
Reep-reep-ree!
Reep-reep-ree!

"Keep up that beat,"
Monkey said to King Frog.
"I thought frogs could only watch and listen."

"Someone's arms and legs may be too short to play or dance. But they can use their voices, no matter how different they may sound," said Crane.

"I guess everyone has something to add when it comes to making music," King Frog croaked.

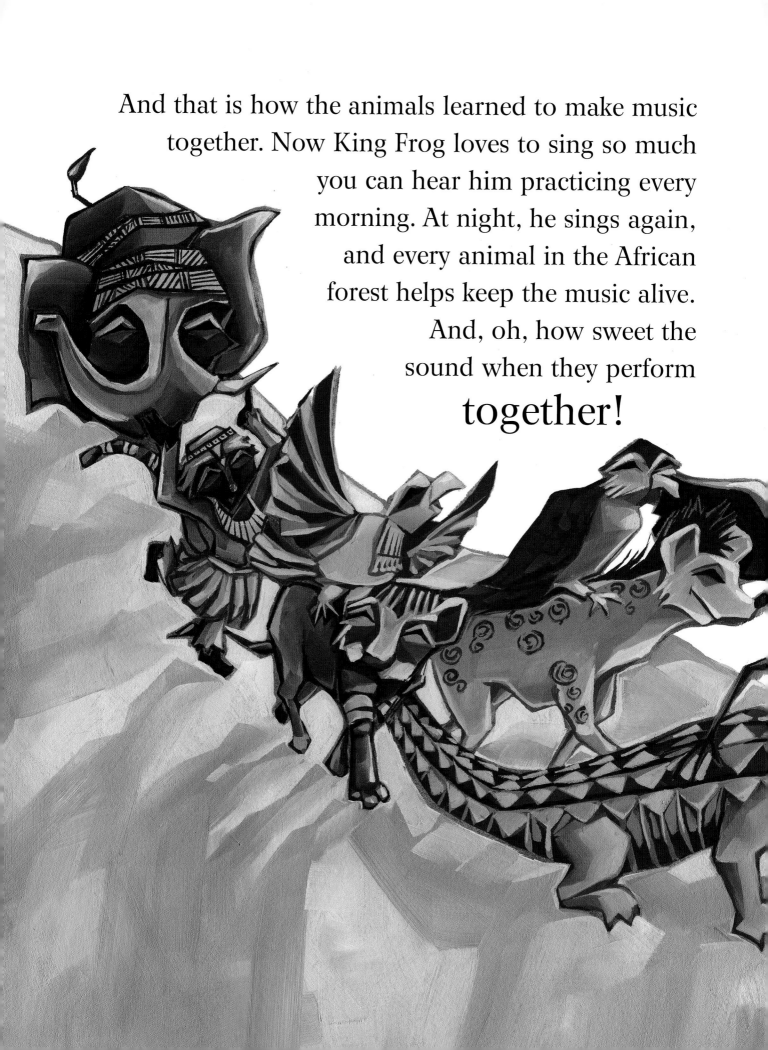

And that is how the animals learned to make music together. Now King Frog loves to sing so much you can hear him practicing every morning. At night, he sings again, and every animal in the African forest helps keep the music alive. And, oh, how sweet the sound when they perform **together!**

Padada BOOM—pada BOOM—
       padada BOOM—pada BOOM!

Shh-ka-shh! Shh-ka-shh! Shh-ka-shh!
Shh-ka-shh! Skee-de-lee! Kee-key-key!
       Skee-de-lee! Kee-key-key!

       Reep-reep-ree!
       Reep-reep-ree!
       Reep-reep-ree!

       Pada **BOOM!**
              BOOM!

Author's Note

Africa enthralls me. My curiosity about its culture took me there; the people, music, and feeling of being home keeps me there. When I returned from my first trip there, storytelling was no longer something to do from head to mouth, but rather an art form filled with heartfelt purpose in teaching children of all ages. I knew that sharing and telling stories was what I wanted to do as my life's work.

Without stories we would have no way of passing on our history and lessons learned. To hear the rhythm of the story is to be a part of it. *The First Music* was inspired by listening to the pulse of drums, which is constant in the everyday social life in West Africa. I heard the swish of the shakers as leaves on a tree, and the tones of the log drums pierced my ears if I stood too close. I remember also the eerie night-time sounds resounding from a nearby lake. Those are the sounds I heard while in Dakar, Senegal, and Accra, Ghana. These sounds are part of everyday life there and were the same sounds our ancestors first heard. Those were the sounds that the human ear heard as its very first music!

As you read my story, make sure to let the children experience those sounds as they, too, hear what their ancestors first heard. Let them pound with Elephant, sway and swish with Monkey, and sing as creakingly as the Frogs. Take some time between pages and let the illustrations help guide the movement and the merriment. Just have fun as you read! Because the children, too, will have something special to add when it comes to us, together, making beautiful music! And, oh, how sweet it will sound!

—DP